The
Mystery
Man

Margaret Ryan
Illustrated by Sholto Walker

RIGBY

Chapter 1

Brownhill was a very ordinary street. It had ordinary gardens, ordinary houses, and ordinary people living there.

Samuel Green didn't think the street was ordinary. He was always making up amazing stories about the people who lived there.

For instance, Sam was sure that Miss Kowlinsky, who lived in the big, red house, was really a secret spy because she always wore dark glasses.

He was sure that Mr Olson, who lived at the end of the street, was really a famous skier because he always wore a ski hat.

And, when Mr Groggs moved in next door to the Green family, Sam was sure he was really a burglar.

"Does Mr Groggs have BURGLAR written in big letters on his forehead?" laughed Sam's big sister, Lucy.

"No," said Sam, "but he does have a droopy, black moustache."

"So does Uncle Mark," laughed Sam's mum, "and he's a dentist! I'm sure Mr Groggs is just an ordinary man. We must invite him over for coffee one day and welcome him to the area."

"Not until I find out more about him," muttered Sam. "I wonder where he works."

Sam got up very early the next morning.
He peered out of his bedroom window,
hoping to see Mr Groggs going to work. He
watched and watched, but Mr Groggs' door
stayed firmly shut.

"Maybe he leaves by the back door,"
thought Sam. "I should have thought of
that earlier."

Sam went into Lucy's room and jumped
up on her bed to look out of the window.

"Who? What? Get off my foot, Sam!"
yelled Lucy.

"Sh! You'll wake Mum and Dad,"
said Sam. "I'm watching for Mr Groggs
to go to work."

"You're crazy," said Lucy, and she
stuck her head back under the covers.

Sam watched for a long time until
he finally saw Mr Groggs. But he
didn't come *out* of the back door,
he went *in*, and he was carrying
something – a big, black torch.

"I knew it," muttered Sam. "I knew there was something strange about Mr Groggs. I bet he *is* a burglar."

Sam moved up the bed to get a better look, until he stood on his sister's pillow.

"Get off, banana brains!" yelled Lucy, and she pushed him to the floor.

"You won't call me that when I've found out more about our mystery man," muttered Sam.

Lucy had already gone back to sleep.

At breakfast time, Sam was sure he knew much more about the mystery man. He had picked up the local paper, and the headline read:

MYSTERY BURGLAR STRIKES AGAIN!

"Listen to this, everyone," said Sam. "It says here that several houses in this area have been robbed and many items stolen. The burglar is reported to have a dark moustache and he carries a torch. That proves it! Mr Groggs is a burglar. I *knew* there was something strange about him."

"Don't be silly," said Sam's dad.

"Mr Groggs is just an ordinary man," said his mum.

"*You're* the one who's strange," said Lucy.

Chapter 2

Sam was sure Mr Groggs was the mystery burglar. Early the next morning he sneaked into Lucy's room and watched for Mr Groggs to return. Sure enough, Mr Groggs appeared carrying the torch and a big, black bag.

"If I could just get a look inside that bag," thought Sam, "I'm sure I could prove that he's the burglar."

Sam woke Lucy. "Come and help me catch the burglar," he said.

"Get lost," muttered Lucy.

"Some help you are," said Sam. He put on his trainers, pulled on a ski hat, just like Mr Olson's, and snuck out of the house. He tiptoed across Mr Groggs' back garden, crept up to the kitchen window, and tried to see in, but the window was too high.

Then Sam saw an old chair. Perfect! He
moved it under the window and climbed up.
Slowly, he raised his head above the window
ledge. There was no sign of Mr Groggs, but
there on the kitchen table was the big,
black bag.

"If I could just look inside it," thought
Sam again, and he leaned further forward.

Then, suddenly, the old chair wobbled and
fell. So did Sam. He yelled as he landed in a
muddy heap on the ground.

The back door opened and Mr Groggs
came out. "Well, well, what have we here?" he
asked.

"Er . . . good morning, Mr Groggs. I'm Samuel
from next door."

"And a very silly boy he is, too," said Sam's
mum, hurrying across the garden.

Sam started to panic. "Um . . . I just came over to invite Mr Groggs for coffee, I mean breakfast."

"No you didn't," said Lucy. "I told Mum and Dad you came over to spy on Mr Groggs. You thought he was the mystery burglar. You thought he had all the stolen stuff in his big, black bag."

Mr Groggs looked cross, but then he started to laugh. "Well, if it'll make you happy, come in and I'll show you what's inside the bag."

They all went in to the kitchen. Mr Groggs opened the big, black bag and Sam looked inside. There was no stolen stuff, but there was . . .

"A kitten!" cried Sam.

"I work the night shift at the Hilltop Animal Shelter," said Mr Groggs. "I take my big torch with me to check up on the animals. Sometimes, some of the animals need extra care. This kitten needs regular feeding, so I had to bring her home with me."

"I suppose I can see how you thought
I might be the burglar, Samuel," said
Mr Groggs. "But you really shouldn't judge
people like that until you know the facts."

"Sorry, Mr Groggs," said Sam. "I didn't mean to be so rude."

"Yes, we're all sorry for Samuel's behaviour," said Mum. "It's just that he's always making up amazing stories about the people on our street."

"He's a nice boy, really," said his dad.

"He's a strange boy, really," said Lucy.

"I really am very sorry, Mr Groggs," said Sam. "Maybe I could weed your garden or something to make up for it?"

"Well, my garden doesn't really need weeding," said Mr Groggs. "But I can think of something you could do to make up for it. We do need a little more help at the animal shelter this week, so perhaps you could come along and help clean out the cages?"

"Clean cages?" cried Sam. "Yuck!"

Lucy laughed. "The perfect job for you, Sam!" she said.

"What a good idea," said Mum. "I can take you up to the shelter after school this week."

"Clean cages?" Sam said again. "Oh, well, I suppose I deserve it."

"You certainly do! Maybe this will teach you to stop making up stories about people," said his mum, and she laughed.

The next day, after school, Sam found himself at the animal shelter, with a broom in his hand. Hilltop was a very ordinary shelter. It had ordinary kennels, ordinary helpers, and ordinary animals staying there.

Samuel Green didn't think the shelter was an ordinary animal shelter. He started making up amazing stories about all the animals that stayed there . . .